Mom...thank you for your unwavering faith and love!

www.mascotbooks.com

Noah Depends on God

For more information, please contact:
Mascot Books
620 Herndon Parkway #320
Herndon, VA 20170
info@mascotbooks.com

Library of Congress Control Number: 2018912235

CPSIA Code: PRT0119A
ISBN-13: 978-1-64307-060-5

Printed in the United States

Noah Depends On God

Lori Long

illustrated by Alejandro Echavez

There once was a man named Noah who listened to God's direction.
He hammered and sawed each day 'til the Ark was built to perfection.

God knew Noah loved Him and knew Noah would obey,
for the world was behaving badly, and this message Noah should relay.

"God will soon be sending forty days and nights of rain."
Everyone just laughed at him. They thought he was insane.

"Change your nasty habits! Turn your hearts back to the Lord!"
But all of Noah's warnings sadly went ignored.

Then all the creatures of this earth, both the great and small,
came two by two as they listened to God's call.

They marched upon the boat in pairs and went where Noah told them.
He gave them all separate quarters, for there was to be no mayhem.

As the rains came down and the waters rose,
Noah and his family were quite busy.
Forty days and forty nights at sea would put
anyone in a tizzy.

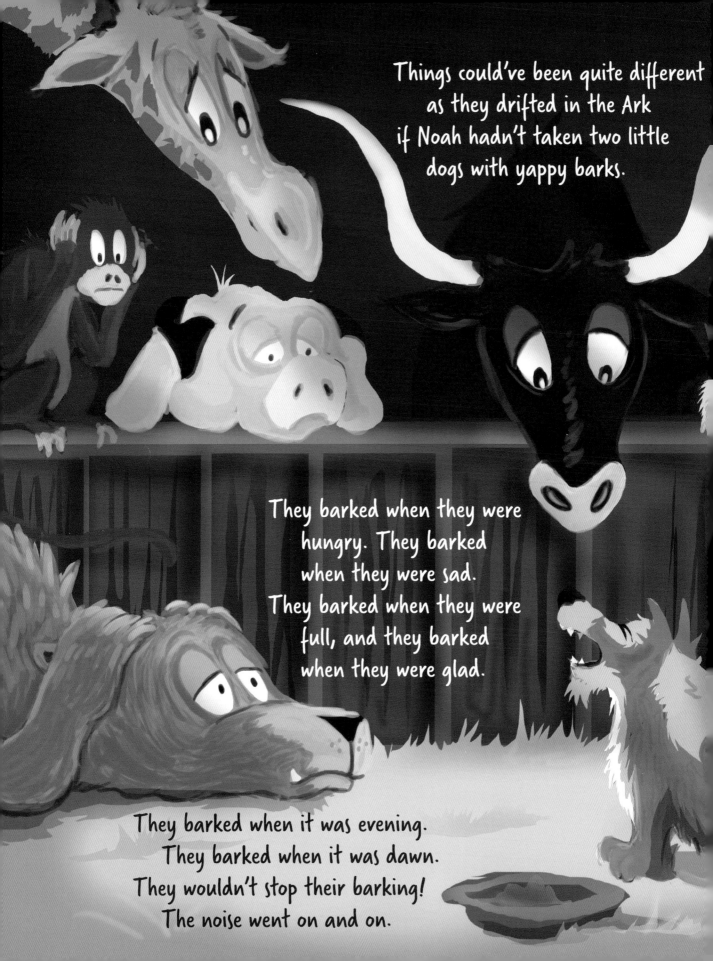

Things could've been quite different
as they drifted in the Ark
if Noah hadn't taken two little
dogs with yappy barks.

They barked when they were
hungry. They barked
when they were sad.
They barked when they were
full, and they barked
when they were glad.

They barked when it was evening.
They barked when it was dawn.
They wouldn't stop their barking!
The noise went on and on.

But one night, as Noah was making his rounds,
he noticed that he didn't hear the usual sounds.

Gone were the little puppies, who never stopped their yapping.
Noah went to check on them, hoping they were just napping.

He hunted for them everywhere.
   Where could those puppies be?
Noah prayed he would find them,
   and they wouldn't be lost at sea.
Noah asked the other animals if
   they had seen the mutts
who barked all day and night, and
   had almost driven them nuts.

As he searched for them everywhere,
ol' Noah got quite worried.
But when he finally found them, the
pair had their little noses buried...

They stood in the pen of the ram with the twisty curly horns.
Why, they had their noses buried in the holes his horns had torn!

"Why you clever little doggies,
       without you we'd be doomed!"
As the waters began receding, their
       endless barking resumed.

A cold, wet nose was given to them for their great deed that day,
for without their loyal watch, Noah and his Ark would've been swept away.

God gave the dogs wet noses to remind us of their devotion,
like the rainbow is God's promise to not flood the world like an ocean.

It's very reassuring to know just as
God spared man,
He also spared the animals, for
we're all part of His plan.

God took care of Noah and the
animals two by two,
and God still cares for you and me.
I'm sure He always knew...

that animals are an example to us of His unconditional love.
They trust in us to provide their needs, as we should in our Father above.

For when we spell "dog" back to
front, it really isn't odd,
that we then spell out the very
name of "God."
I thank my Master up above that
a dog just somehow knows
when it is very important for
him to use his nose.

Sometimes
THE END
is a new
BEGINNING

God gave us animals here on earth, and for
    now they're in our care.
He cares for those who've gone ahead, and we'll
    see them someday there.
God made the heavens and the earth as His
    handiwork unfurled,
and if animals went to a different heaven,
    God would've put them in a different world.

About the Author

Lori was inspired by her love for animals as she wrote this children's story. The author has invited over a dozen (stray and rescue) cats and dogs into her heart and home over the last thirty years. She resides in Pennsylvania with her husband and cat, Stuwee. Most days include visits from her grown son and daughter's four granddogs, who affectionately know her as Graminal.

Your righteousness is like the mighty mountains,
your justice like the ocean depths.
You care for people and animals alike, O Lord.

Psalm 36:6 NLT

About the Illustrator

Alejandro Echavez is a freelance illustrator, painter, and animator specializing in children's illustrations. He currently resides in Long Island, New York, but spent his formative years in Bogotá, Colombia, where he first showed an interest in art at the very young age of 6. More than an interest, it was a natural talent that his family nurtured and developed. His artwork is often colorful and playful in theme. He is not scared of bright colors, which he uses to create movement and vibrancy in his work. Alejandro has worked on several children's books and hopes to continue creating the vivid canvases and artwork he is known for.